Spiritmane and the Hidden Magic

Daisy Meadows

For Ruby and Eliza

Special thanks to Adrian Bott

ORCHARD BOOKS

First published in Great Britain in 2021 by The Watts Publishing Group

1 3 5 7 9 10 8 6 4 2

Text copyright © 2021 Working Partners Limited
Illustrations © Orchard Books 2021
Series created by Working Partners Limited

A CIP catalogue record for this book is available from the British Library.

ISBN 978 1 40836 196 2

Printed and bound in Great Britain by Clays Ltd, Elcograf S.p.A.

The paper and board used in this book are made from wood from responsible sources.

Orchard Books
An imprint of Hachette Children's Group
Part of The Watts Publishing Group Limited
Carmelite House
50 Victoria Embankment
London EC4Y 0DZ

An Hachette UK Company

www.hachette.co.uk
www.hachettechildrens.co.uk

Contents

Meet the Characters

Aisha and Emily are best friends from Spellford Village. Aisha loves sports, whilst Emily's favourite thing is science. But what both girls enjoy more than anything is visiting Enchanted Valley and helping their unicorn friends, who live there.

Quickhoof

The four Sports and Games Unicorns help to make games and competitions fun for everyone. Quickhoof uses her magic locket to help players work well as a team.

Feeling confident in your skills and abilities is so important for sporting success. Brightblaze's magic helps to make sure everyone believes in themselves!

Brightblaze

Fairtail

Games are no fun when players cheat or don't follow the rules. Fairtail's magic locket reminds everyone to play fair!

When things get difficult, Spiritmane's perseverance locket gives sportspeople the strength to face their challenges and succeed.

Spiritmane

Spellford

Enchanted Valley

Enchanted Cottage

Golden Palace

An Enchanted Valley lies a twinkle away,
Where beautiful unicorns live, laugh and play
You can visit the mermaids, or go for a ride,
So much fun to be had, but dangers can hide!

Your friends need your help – this is how you know:
A keyring lights up with a magical glow.
Whirled off like a dream, you won't want to leave.
Friendship forever, when you truly believe.

Chapter One
School Day Surprise

Emily Turner sat next to her best friend, Aisha Khan, and kicked her heels against her chair. Why did the last few minutes of school always seem to take for ever?

Emily loved school, but she couldn't wait for the weekend to begin. She looked out of the window and sighed.

She wished she was already in the park, learning some new football moves from Aisha.

The clock on the classroom wall was almost at three. The second hand counted down. Five, four, three, two …

Bringggg! Finally, the bell! Chairs

scraped on the floor as everyone scrambled out of their seats.

"Have a lovely weekend, everyone, and don't forget your homework!" called Miss Mayhew above the noise, as everyone stuffed their pencil cases back into their bags.

Emily began to pack away … and then stopped. Where was her favourite pencil? The pink one with the unicorn at the end? It *always* sat at the top of her desk. But it wasn't there now.

"Oh no!" she groaned. She quickly checked her pencil case.

"What's wrong?" Aisha asked.

"I've lost my unicorn pencil," Emily said to her friend. "The one you gave me for my birthday!"

Both Emily and Aisha loved unicorns. And they shared a special unicorn secret too.

"Don't worry," Aisha said. "I bet it's just

rolled off the desk."

They peered under the desks and between the chair legs. All the other children were already hurrying out of the classroom, Miss Mayhew following behind.

On the floor, the girls found a hair elastic, a chewing-gum wrapper and plenty of dust, but Emily's unicorn pencil was nowhere to be seen.

"It can't have just vanished into thin air," Aisha said, getting to her feet and looking around.

Emily sighed. "Well, we won't find it now. Let's go home."

At the last moment, she decided to check her pocket. The pencil wasn't there,

but something
inside was shining.

"Aisha,
my keyring's
glowing!" Emily
said.

Aisha pulled her
own keyring out.
"So's mine!"

Both girls

were lucky enough to own beautiful
crystal keyrings in the shape of unicorns.
This was the special secret they shared.
When the keyrings lit up, it meant their
unicorn friend – Queen Aurora – was
calling them. Queen Aurora ruled over
Enchanted Valley, a magical place where

unicorns lived, along with many other strange and wonderful creatures.

Even though it was time for the girls to go home from school, they knew they could travel to Enchanted Valley. In the ordinary world, time stood still while they were away. Still, they didn't want anyone spotting them going off on their adventure!

"We'd better hide," Aisha said. "Miss Mayhew might come back any minute now."

They dashed out of the classroom, looking around. Across the corridor was a supply cupboard where they wouldn't be seen. They ran over and opened the door to scramble inside.

In the dark of the cupboard, Aisha and Emily held up their keyrings and touched the tips of the unicorn horns together.

At once, a whirling spiral of multi-coloured sparkles whooshed up around them. As the rainbow twinkles swirled before their eyes, their feet rose up from the floor. The girls floated in the air and the school cupboard vanished like a mist. The world seemed to hold its breath …

Next moment, the sparkles faded away and their feet sank down again. They were standing on the lush grass of Enchanted Valley. Nearby, on top of a hill, was Queen Aurora's castle, with its four golden towers shaped like unicorn horns. Around it was a moat of blue water.

Right in front of them stood a huge silver stadium. Flags, pennants and ribbons fluttered from poles sticking up from the roof.

"The Enchanted Valley Games!" Emily cried, with a flutter of excitement. "They must be almost ready to start."

The girls knew about the Games from their recent visits to the valley. Creatures

were going to come from all over Enchanted Valley to compete in every event imaginable! Lots of different sports and games were included, from chess to volleyball, and they all had a magical twist. You could play a game of snap against a friendly crocodile, or bounce on magical trampolines that sent you up into the clouds!

Emily and Aisha had been looking forward to the Games, but the unicorns hadn't been able to begin them yet, because of a wicked unicorn called Selena.

"I hope Selena hasn't been causing any more trouble," murmured Aisha as they walked towards the stadium.

Selena had stolen the magical lockets
of the four Sports and Games Unicorns,
and refused to give them back unless
the unicorns made her queen. Until the
lockets were all found and returned,
the Games couldn't begin. The girls
had already helped Quickhoof get her
Teamwork locket, Brightblaze retrieve her
Confidence locket and Fairtail find her
Sportsmanship locket. They knew there
was still one locket left to return.

As they drew closer to the stadium, they
saw a terrible sight. It was being taken
to pieces! A group of badgers in overalls
pushed wheelbarrows, carrying bits of the
stadium away. Magpies took down the
banners. Unicorns and other creatures

packed away all the sports and games
equipment.

"Oh no! I think we've missed the
Games!" Emily wailed.

Aisha pointed. "Look! There's Queen
Aurora," she said. "She'll know what's
going on."

Queen Aurora walked towards them.
Her coat shimmered with all the
beautiful colours of the dawn, but her
head hung and her tail drooped.

"Are we too late for the Games?" Emily asked.

"No," sighed Queen Aurora. "The Games are cancelled. I'm sorry to say that Selena has won."

"What?" both girls cried.

Queen Aurora's eyes brimmed with tears. "I called you here to thank you for helping me so many times. But I won't ask for your help any more. It's all over. After today, I shall rule Enchanted Valley no more. Selena will be queen."

Aisha and Emily looked at one another.

"H–how can you say that?" Aisha stammered. "How can you just give up?"

"I'm sorry," Queen Aurora said. "There's nothing I can do."

Emily grabbed Aisha's arm. "Hold on. Spiritmane's locket is still missing, isn't it? And it's the Perseverance locket – the one that gives you the power to keep going. No wonder Queen Aurora wants to give up!"

"Of course," Aisha said. "She's lost her power to stay determined! We need to find Spiritmane, and fast."

Chapter Two
Queen Selena the First

The girls soon caught sight of Spiritmane, with her lavender-coloured body and her creamy mane and tail. She was looking on miserably as the badgers took a golden podium to bits.

"Not much point in having a winners' podium if there aren't going to be any

Games," she sighed.

The three other Sports and Games Unicorns nodded. Emily recognised Quickhoof, Brightblaze and Fairtail.

Emily and Aisha ran over to their friends.

"Spiritmane, it's us! We've come to help!" called Emily.

"Don't give up. We'll get your locket back," added Aisha.

"Hmm? Oh, hello," said Spiritmane, giving them a sad smile. "Don't bother trying to find my locket. It's gone for good."

A heap of footballs had been left by the podium. Spiritmane began to nudge them into an open sack. "We won't need these any more," she muttered.

"Oof!" said a squeaky voice from inside the sack. A little hamster tumbled out!

He landed right in front of Emily and Aisha, and blinked. Then he sprang up and dusted himself off. "Hello!" he said, grinning. "Did I vin?"

"Vin?" Aisha asked, puzzled.

"Vin!" the hamster repeated. "Opposite of lose!"

"Er … win what?" said Aisha.

"The hide and seek practice, vot else?" squeaked the hamster.

Emily and Aisha looked at the funny little animal grinning up at them. It was an oddly *pointy* grin. To Emily's surprise, she saw the hamster had two tiny fangs!

"I'm sorry, but you didn't win," Spiritmane told him. "Practice was cancelled. So were the rest of the Games. Everyone's going home."

"Cancelled?" The hamster's face fell. "After I spent so long hiding in that sack? Drat. Vot a shame." He looked up at the girls, and his face lit up again. "Ah! Vhere are my manners? You two must be Aisha and Emily!"

"That's right," said Emily, smiling warmly. "But who are you?"

The little hamster swelled up with pride. "I … am Spike. And I'm a vampster!"

Two tiny bat wings unfurled from Spike's back.

Aisha covered her mouth so she wouldn't giggle. "I'm sorry, but … what's a vampster?"

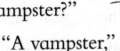

"A vampster," Spiritmane said, "is a vampire hamster."

"Don't be scared!" Spike said, with a fangy smile. "I only eat blood oranges!"

He vanished back inside the sack of footballs and came out a second later, pulling a bag of blood oranges behind him. "I am a hide and seek champion," he explained. "Sometimes, vhen I need to hide for a long time, I bring a snack along to keep me going. *I vant to suck your blood* … orange."

He sank his fangs into one and slurped. "Yum. So juicy!"

Aisha and Emily grinned at one another. They were both thinking the same thing: there was nothing *less* scary than the little vampster. He was about as frightening as a cuddly toy!

Spiritmane said, "Spike really *is* the hide and seek champion of Enchanted Valley.

Whether he's hiding or seeking, he just doesn't give up. He's never been beaten!"

"You are too kind, my friend," Spike said. "I just do my best."

Next moment, there was a blinding flash of lightning and a huge *kaboom* of thunder.

In the middle of the stadium appeared a silver unicorn, with a mane and tail of electric blue. She looked at the creatures surrounding her and laughed.

"Selena!" Emily gasped.

"And she's got Grubb with her, as usual," muttered Aisha. Grubb was Selena's grey, lumpy ogre servant.

"Hello, you fools!" jeered Selena. "Oh, look, those two annoying girls are here.

After the locket, are you? You might as well give up, because you're not getting it back!" She turned to Aurora. "Of course, if you make me queen, I might let you have it …"

"Very well, Selena," said Queen Aurora, shaking her head sadly. "You win. Meet me at the palace at noon and I will hand over the crown to you."

"At last!" Selena crowed. "Long live Queen Selena the First!"

"No way," said Emily, her hands on her hips.

"*We're* not giving up," said Aisha. "And you'll never be queen."

Selena made a face. "So, you're still trying to stop me?" she said. "Fine. I'll just hide the locket somewhere you will never find it."

"Oh, vonderful!" piped up Spike. "Hide and seek is my favourite game. I like a challenge."

"Spike always wins," said Emily firmly, jutting her chin out at Selena. "And he's on our side."

"Yeah, he's a champion!" said Aisha.

Selena glared at Spike. "A pipsqueak like you, a champion? Well then, game on, you ghoulish gerbil! I'm going to hide this locket. If you can't find it before high noon, the crown is mine. I'll be Queen of Enchanted Valley for ever!"

"I want to hide the locket!" Grubb shouted and stomped his stony foot. "Maybe then I can win something."

Selena rolled her eyes. "Very well,

Grubb! Now, come on. We're leaving."

Grubb grabbed Spike's bag of blood oranges.

"Hey!" yelled Spike.

"Yum!" Grubb said. "Thanks for the treat."

With another crash of thunder and blaze of light, Selena was gone, and Grubb ran off into the distance.

Spike sagged, like a balloon the week after a birthday party. "Ah. On second thoughts … perhaps I can't do this," he said.

"But you're the champion!" Emily said.

"But ve are already halfway through the morning," Spike groaned. "How on earth are ve going to search all of Enchanted Valley before noon? Maybe ve should just give up now."

"He's right, you know," Queen Aurora added gloomily.

Emily whispered to Aisha: "This is all because the Perseverance locket is gone! Even Spike's feeling the effect now."

Aisha nodded. "We've only just arrived, so we're not feeling it yet. But all the creatures in Enchanted Valley have been missing their perseverance for days."

"I bet Spike can still help us, though, even if he doesn't believe it," said Emily.

"Hmm," Aisha said. "Before a football match, our coach always gives us a pep talk. It really helps us stay positive. Maybe I should give one to Spike?"

"Brilliant idea!" Emily grinned.

Aisha bent down. "Hey, Spike? I know you like winning. We all do. But it's not all about winning the game, is it? It's

about having a go and doing your best."

"That's right," added Emily. "Every time you play a game, there is a chance you won't win. But if you don't play, you *definitely* won't win."

Spike gave them a little smile. "You may be young, but you show great visdom," he said.

He stood up and spread his wings. "The challenge may be great," he said, "but I, Spike the Vampster, will try my best!"

The girls' pep talk had worked. The game was on!

Chapter Three
The Peel Trail

Emily put her arm around Spiritmane's neck. "You should come too," she told her friend.

"I think my locket's gone for ever, and we'll never find it," said Spiritmane sadly. "But I suppose I'd better come with you."

"Velcome to the team!" cheered Spike.

"I think I'll go back to the palace," Queen Aurora said wearily. "I'll say goodbye to it one last time."

"Don't give up, Your Highness!" Aisha urged.

"Yes, you go to the palace and make sure Selena doesn't move herself in," said Emily. "It's still yours!"

Aurora nodded. "For now," she said. She turned and began to walk slowly up the hill towards the palace.

"I can't bear to see Queen Aurora feeling so hopeless. We must find that locket," said Emily.

They headed for the big arched doorway that led out of the stadium. Some banners had been hung up above the door, and a group of kittens with butterfly wings were taking them down.

"Look, kitterflies!" Aisha said, pointing.

"Yes, there's Minky," said Emily, waving to a black and white kitterfly who they had met on a previous adventure.

A little kitterfly with buttercup-yellow wings let go of her banner. She gave a sigh as it fluttered to the ground. "This is taking ages," she said. "Let's just give up."

"Good idea," said Minky. "What's the point of taking all this stuff down, anyway? It'll fall down by itself eventually."

Emily gave Aisha a worried look. "Oh dear. They can't even persevere with giving up!"

"We need to find that locket before things get worse," said Aisha.

"Where should we start looking?" wondered Emily.

"Let's ask the hide and seek champion!" Aisha said. "Spike, where do you think Grubb might be hiding?"

"I always check the most obvious place first," said Spike. "Just in case!"

"I suppose the most obvious place is

right here by the stadium," said Emily.

They all began to search, around the trees, under the benches and along the side of the path. Nobody found anything, until …

"Vait!" Spike narrowed his beady eyes and swooped down on something lying on the ground.

"That looks like peel from a blood orange," Aisha said.

"It is!" Emily said. "But what's it doing out here on the grass?"

Spike frowned. "It looks like one of mine. But I don't peel my oranges, I just sink my fangs into them!"

"Besides, Spike always puts his rubbish in the bin," added Spiritmane.

Aisha snapped her fingers. "I've got it. Grubb must have dropped that orange peel. He stole that big bag of oranges from you, and it's just like him to leave litter lying about on the ground. He must have come this way!"

Spiritmane and Spike looked at one another doubtfully.

Just then, Aisha caught sight of another little piece of peel, lying in the grass up ahead. "Look!"

"That silly ogre's left a trail for us to follow," laughed Emily.

"See? We *can* do this! Come on!" Aisha cried.

The trail of dropped orange peel led away from the stadium, over a green grassy hill and down through a wide, echoing valley. Following the trail, they found a huge ogre footprint, and grinned at one another. They'd catch up with Grubb in no time!

But then they reached a pile of peel, and they couldn't see another piece anywhere.

There was nothing else around, except for a mound of muddy earth that looked a bit like a heap of mashed potatoes covered with gravy.

"What do we do now?!" Aisha cried.

Emily searched around, and her eyes fixed on the mound of mud. It must be a house, she realised, because a wonky door was stuck in the middle of it. Next to the house was a rubbish heap. If it hadn't been for the door, it might have been hard to tell the house from the rubbish.

A wooden sign stood outside the house, with writing scrawled on it in dribbly black paint.

Emily got closer and read the sign.

NOT Welcome to Grubb's House.

"Charming!" said Spike, reading it too.

"He must be in there," said Spiritmane. "Let's sneak up quietly."

They crept close. Emily bent down and peered in through a crack in the wall. "I can't see Grubb," she said.

"What about my locket? Can you see it?" Spiritmane asked.

Emily said, "There's something at the back of the burrow, and it's all sparkly!

But it's really dark in there."

Spike flapped up. "I am the only one small enough to get through that crack," he said bravely. "Even if it's all a vaste of time, I must try!"

The little vampster climbed in through the tiny hole. Aisha and Emily held their breath.

Moments later, they heard Spike's muffled voice: "Ooh, it's smelly in here! There's old ogre socks and a mouldy sandvich."

"Can you see the locket?" Emily called.

The only answer was a rustling noise as Spike rummaged through Grubb's things.

Suddenly, Spike popped out of the crack! On his face was a big grin, and in his paws was a glittering locket with a picture of a scroll. "Ta-daaah!" he squeaked.

"My locket!" gasped Spiritmane.

"Well done, Spike!" the girls cheered.

They hugged him – very gently, because he was so small – and Spike puffed up with pride.

"I'm still the hide and seek champion," he said happily.

"That's brilliant," said Aisha, "and better still, it's not even high noon yet! We've

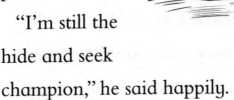

won!"

Emily cried, "Selena won't be queen after all! Long live Queen Aurora!" Her triumphant shout echoed through the land.

"Who's that shouting?" said a gruff voice. From over by the rubbish heap came a groaning, rumbling, grumbling noise, like a whale with a tummy ache. Suddenly, a big boulder stood up.

The boulder glared at them with large round eyes. It wasn't a boulder at all. It was Grubb, disguised as a rock!

"Where did you come from?" he roared. "You must have sneaked right past me!"

He charged at Spike, but the little vampster flew up into the air. "Let's put this locket back where it belongs," he said.

"No!" Grubb shouted, and reached out for Spike.

But Spike's bat wings whirred and he flew over to Spiritmane. She bowed her head. Spike quickly hung the locket around her neck.

"No!" Grubb cried again. "Selena will be furious with me." He sounded very pathetic.

Emily and Aisha watched, smiling, and waited for Spiritmane's magic to return.

But nothing happened. Spiritmane looked just as sad as before.

"Why isn't it working?" murmured Aisha.

"My magic's gone," said Spiritmane in a hollow voice. "It's gone for good. The crown is lost. There's only one thing left to do now."

"What's that?" Emily cried.

Spiritmane sank to the ground, put her head on her hooves and closed her eyes. "Give up."

Chapter Four
Selena's Locket Switch

A frown came over Spike's little furry face. "Does this mean I didn't vin after all? I don't understand. I *alvays* vin."

Emily bent down to take a better look at the locket. As she held it in her hand, flaky gold paint rubbed off on her fingers. In fact, now she could see it in the light, it looked like something from a Christmas cracker.

"This isn't Spiritmane's locket at all," she said. "It's a fake!"

Aisha said, "Selena must have given Grubb a fake locket to hide and kept the real locket for herself."

Grubb howled. "Selena tricked me!" He stamped his foot and the ground shook.

"Yes, she did," Emily said.

Grubb sat down on a rock. His bottom lip stuck out. "Why would she do that? I thought she was letting me play hide and seek. But it was all a big lie!"

"I'm sorry, Grubb, but that's what Selena's like," Aisha said. "She tricks people. Even when you think she's on your side."

"Hmm," said Grubb, and rested his huge chin on his fist. He furrowed his brow, deep in thought.

Emily was a little surprised. She'd never seen Grubb look thoughtful before.

Spiritmane shrugged the fake locket off and threw it on to Grubb's enormous rubbish heap. "We've wasted the whole morning looking for a locket that wasn't even real," she said. "The sun's almost overhead, and then it'll be noon. Soon it will be too late!"

"Selena's going to be queen, then. I suppose ve'd better get used to it," said Spike miserably. "I don't expect it'll be much fun. She probably von't let anyone else vin any games."

"No," Grubb said. He heaved a massive sigh. "I wish I'd never helped her in the first place! You girls had the right idea, trying to stop her all the time. I bet there won't be any more games for anyone, except for her."

Emily turned pale. "Aisha," she said. 'I've just had a thought. It's Aurora's magic that brings us here, but if she's not queen any more ... What if we can never come back to Enchanted Valley again?"

Aisha gasped. "You're right! We can

only travel here because of the power of Aurora's friendship. Without that, we won't ever see any of our friends again!"

The thought was like a rain cloud covering up the sun. Emily suddenly felt like giving up.

That must be because the locket is gone, she thought. *This is what everyone else is already feeling. Soon I'll be as sad as Spiritmane and Spike.*

"I'm going to miss Enchanted Valley so much," Aisha said, with a trembling voice.

"We hardly knew each other when we first came," Emily said. "But look at us now. Our mums say we're like twins! Enchanted Valley really helped bring us together, didn't it?"

"Yes! But it's not just the two of us, it's everyone else too!" said Aisha. "Aurora and Hob and Pearl, and all the others … Milo the Moonwolf, and Prism, and Fluffy … Oh, we've had so many adventures here. And all because we've been making new friends, all the time!"

Bright light suddenly blazed from the girls' pockets. It shone so strongly you could even see it through the fabric!

"Our keyrings?" said Emily. "But …
we're already here in Enchanted Valley.
What's going on?"

They both took out their keyrings
and looked at them. They were glowing,
bright as the morning sun.

"They've never glowed while we were
in Enchanted Valley before," Aisha said.

Emily held her friend's hand tight. "It's
a sign from Queen Aurora. It has to be!
She's trying to tell us something!"

The two girls both realised what
Aurora's message had to be.

Aisha said: "Even if it's hopeless …"

And Emily said: "And even if there's no
way to win …"

Together they said, "We'll never give up

on our friendship!"

They hugged one another like they wouldn't ever let go.

"We have to keep fighting," said Aisha.

"And if there's no hope to be found, we'll just have to *make* some," said Emily.

Aisha turned to Spiritmane and Spike. She forced down the despair she could feel. "Come on!" she said brightly. "Why don't we see this as a new game? Us four versus Selena. And the prize is Enchanted Valley!"

"Us *five*!" bellowed Grubb suddenly.

Everyone turned and stared.

Grubb whispered to Spike, "Um … five does come after four, doesn't it?"

Spike nodded. Grubb stood up and came

over to the girls.

"I want to join your team, if you'll have me," he said. "I want to help put things right. It's not too late, is it?"

"Of course you can join us, Grubb!" said Aisha. "We'd be glad to have you!"

"It's *never* too late," added Emily with a grin. "Not when you have your friends by your side."

Chapter Five
Quaking Quarry

"So where should we start looking?" Spiritmane asked. And the girls were glad to see she hadn't completely given up yet.

"Hmm," said Emily, looking round. "This is going to be tricky. There's no trail to follow."

"Selena might have left hoof prints,"

suggested Aisha. "And she always makes storm clouds when she flies around, doesn't she? Let's look for both of those."

Emily and Aisha shielded their eyes from the sun as they peered up into the sky. The others carefully searched the ground.

Emily had a sudden thought. "Hey, Grubb? Can you think of anything

Selena might have said about her plan?"

Grubb screwed up his face, frowned hard and scratched his ear. He was clearly thinking very, very hard.

Slowly, he said, "I remember … Selena asked me how I disguise myself as a rock. I showed her how to do it."

"So how *do* you do it?" Emily asked.

"Well," said Grubb, looking proud of himself, "you find a load of rocks. Then you lie down on the ground, and you sort of … roll around a bit."

"How does that help?" Spike asked.

"It covers you with dirt and moss!" Grubb explained. "I'm already greyish and a bit lumpy, so I have a head start, you see? Then you curl up into a ball, and keep as still as you can."

Aisha put a finger on her chin. "I wonder … Maybe Selena asked Grubb about his disguise because she wanted to copy it!"

"Could Selena be hiding somewhere in Enchanted Valley, disguised as a rock?" cried Emily.

Spike suddenly became excited. "I think I know where she might be. Follow me!"

Off Spike flew. Grubb followed, thundering through the valley with great bounding strides. Everyone hurried to keep up with them.

As the girls passed underneath the branches of a tree, they heard voices

coming from a nest.

"I don't want to do my flying lessons any more, Mum," piped a tiny voice.

Emily glanced up and saw a baby bluebird peeping over the edge.

"I'm rubbish at flying," the bluebird sighed. "I'll never learn. What's the point in carrying on?"

Further on, Aisha saw smoke curling up

from a little cave mouth in the side of a hill. Out came a small dragon in a white apron, carrying a mixing bowl with a spoon stuck in it.

"What a waste of time!" the dragon cried, and angrily banged the bowl down on a tree stump. "Why should I bother making Rory Firefiddle a birthday cake, anyway? I'll probably just burn it, and he won't want to be my friend any more. I'm giving up."

Emily and Aisha shared a worried glance. "Uh-oh," Emily said. "Things are getting worse."

"People are giving up on everything, not just on sports and games," said Aisha. "We have to get Spiritmane's locket back!"

"Almost there," puffed Grubb. "Just at the top of this big hill …"

The girls followed him up to the very

top. But what they found there took them by surprise. Instead of soft green grass, the ground dropped away into a great rocky hollow. There were rocks of all shapes, sizes and colours lying around. Some were even gold and silver.

"Vatch out," Spike warned, as they climbed into it. "This is the Quaking Quarry, the rockiest place in the land. If you vanted to hide in a rock disguise, this

is the place to do it. The ground can go a bit vibbly-vobbly sometimes, so be careful how you step."

Aisha and Emily looked out over the quarry, trying to spot any rock that might be Selena in disguise.

"If she is hiding somewhere here, it won't be easy to find her," Aisha agreed.

Spiritmane said, "Selena can use magic, too. So she might have used it to make her disguise even better." She hung her head. "If there even *is* a disguise. She's probably not even here. She could be miles away by now. Look at the sky – it's almost noon. We might as well just give up."

Aisha stroked Spiritmane gently. "No.

We've come this far, and we've nothing to lose by trying just a bit longer."

But as she looked from rock to rock for any sign of Selena, she began to feel hopelessness creeping in. There were just so many rocks!

"I wish the Quaking Quarry would hurry up and quake," Emily said. "If this place was full of rocks tumbling about, I bet Selena would fly out of the way and show herself."

Grubb's face lit up. "Great idea! Everyone, stand back!"

Grubb charged down into the quarry.

Then he started dancing. He jumped and clapped and stomped his huge feet.

"Woohoo!" he yelled. "Rompy stompy!"

He did a back flip and came down hard on his bottom. The ground underneath him began to quake and then the whole quarry started shaking. Emily and Aisha ducked as rocks went

tumbling past them.

"Quick!" Spiritmane said. "Climb aboard!"

The girls scrambled on to Spiritmane's back. She leapt into the air, safely out of the way of the flying rocks. Spike fluttered nearby.

The quarry shook harder. Rocks
whizzed back and forth.

"Look!" Emily cried with delight.
"There she is!"

A big silvery rock uncurled itself. It was
Selena!

Chapter Six
Friendship Power!

With a panicked screech, Selena shot up into the air. A boulder crashed down right on the spot where she'd been a moment before.

Aisha hugged Spiritmane's neck. "See? I knew we mustn't give up!"

Selena scowled down at them. Her eyes

flashed with anger. Around her neck hung a sparkling locket with a picture of a scroll on it. "You! I should have known!" she roared.

"My locket!" Silvermane said.

Selena yelled, "You little fools! Why aren't you giving up yet? Can't you see I've already won?"

"Not yet, you haven't!" Emily yelled back.

"And we'll never give up!" Aisha shouted. "Don't you see? You might have stolen the locket's magic, but we've something even more powerful. Our friendship!"

Emily said, "We had it all along, we just didn't realise until now. Look! Grubb's our friend now, too."

"Oh, is he indeed?" Selena snarled. She looked down at Grubb. "I should have known you'd betray me. You're the worst servant I ever had!" Lightning flickered in her eyes as she reared up angrily. "You'll be sorry, you worthless ogre!"

"I'm already sorry!" Grubb shouted, and stamped his foot. "Sorry I ever helped you! You're nothing but a … a nasty old meanie-pants. I hope you never get to be queen!"

As Selena launched into another angry speech about how hopeless Grubb was, Spike beckoned Emily and Aisha to lean in close. He whispered, "Can you keep

 Selena busy?"

"I think so," said Emily. "Why, do you have a plan?"

"Yes!" Spike grinned. "Vhile she's not looking,

I can fly round behind her and vhisk that locket right off her neck!"

Aisha and Emily shared a worried glance. "That sounds really dangerous, Spike," said Aisha.

"If Selena catches you, she'll be furious," added Emily. "Are you sure you want to go through with it?"

"Yes," Spike said bravely. "You vould not give up on your friends, so I shall not give up on mine! Even if it feels like there is no hope, I must do my best."

Spiritmane flew the girls down next to Grubb. Aisha leaned over and whispered into his ear, "We need you to distract Selena so Spike can steal the locket."

Grubb nodded. "Leave it to me. I know

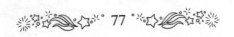

just what to do."

He marched up in front of Selena, threw himself down on the ground and started beating his fists. "It's not fair!" he roared. "You wouldn't even let me hide the real locket!"

"Stop that at once, you silly ogre," Selena snapped. "You'll start another earthquake!"

But the earthquake had already begun

– and it was even bigger than the first one. All around, huge rocks bounced up into the air. Even the boulders at the very top of the quarry started to tumble down. The more Grubb pounded the ground, the more rocks went rolling down.

"Eek!" Selena squealed. She dodged, yelping as the boulders shot past her. Meanwhile, Spike fluttered round behind her with his little bat wings.

Selena was distracted. Spike reached out to snatch the locket. Emily and Aisha held their breath. Closer … closer … almost there …

Just as Spike was about to grab the chain of the locket, Selena turned and stared right at him!

"Oh no!" the girls said together.

Selena narrowed her eyes. There was a sudden, brilliant, silvery-blue flash. With a *boomf*, a little grey storm cloud appeared. And Spike was caught inside it!

The little vampster couldn't move his wings. All he could do was hang helplessly

inside the cloud, while Selena glared at him. "So! Thought you could trick me, did you?" She laughed evilly. "Well, it's nearly noon. Nearly time to crown me as queen!"

Emily and Aisha gulped. It might really all be over now. There seemed no hope left at all. They might as well give up.

Chapter Seven
Sticky Attack!

"Silly little meddling vampster!" Selena mocked. "Did you really think it would be this easy to beat me?"

Spike glared back at her. "I don't care how hard it is. Ve *vill* beat you. And I vill never give up!"

Selena threw back her head and

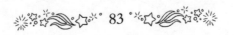

laughed. "Neither will I!"

"And neither will I!" Grubb shouted.

Quick as a flash, he pulled out the
rest of the blood oranges he'd stolen. He
held them up in his big, lumpy fist and
squeezed.

SPLOOSH! All the juice exploded out
of the oranges at once – and most of it
went over Selena!

"ARGH!" Selena shrieked as the juice dribbled down her face. "Disgusting! Sticky!" She thrashed her head around and screwed her eyes up tight. "My lovely mane's ruined! And now it's in my eye! Ooh, it stings!!"

The storm cloud vanished with a pop. Spike's wings were suddenly free. He swooped down, caught hold of the locket, and whisked it off Selena's neck.

"Give that back!" Selena shouted. "Pesky rodent! Where are you?" Her eyes were still covered with orange juice. "Ouch!"

Spike darted away, leaving Selena helpless and sticky. The little vampster quickly flew to Spiritmane and lowered the locket around her neck.

Spiritmane stood up straight. It was as if the light came back into her eyes.

"Thank you," she whispered.

"Hooray!" Emily and Aisha cheered. Spike beamed, and Grubb happily clapped his huge hands together.

"We did it!" cried Emily.

Aisha looked around, smiling. "Well done, everyone!"

There was a tiny boom of thunder. A black thundercloud appeared over Selena, and began to rain. It washed the juice away, but left her looking like a bedraggled old mop.

"I'll get my revenge on all of you," she growled. "Especially, you, Grubb! I'd make a much better queen than Aurora. You'll see. I'll keep coming back, and one day, I'll win!"

"You know," Spiritmane said thoughtfully, "I usually tell people *not* to give up. But in your case …"

"Give up now!" Aisha and Emily finished.

Everyone laughed except for Selena, who stamped her hoof in fury. Then she flew off into the sky. Thunder grumbled for a moment, then she was gone.

"Follow us, Grubb!" Spiritmane said.

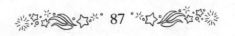

"Why? Where are we going?" Grubb asked.

"The stadium, of course!" Spiritmane said, laughing. "The Enchanted Valley Games are back on."

Moments later, they swept down from the sky towards the stadium. A huge crowd was waving and cheering.

Over the entrance, the kitterflies

were putting a banner back up. "Keep going! We can do it!" said Minky as she struggled to fix her end in place.

The crowd made space for Spiritmane to land and the girls slid off her back. Queen Aurora came bounding up, bright as the dawning sun.

She nuzzled Emily and Aisha fondly. "Thank you for never giving up," she said.

"You've won. Enchanted Valley is safe!"

The girls hugged her, and all the creatures burst into applause.

"Oh! I meant to ask," Emily said. "Back then, just when everything seemed like it couldn't get any worse, our keyrings glowed!"

"It was like a sign that we shouldn't give up," said Aisha. "Was that you, sending us a message?"

Queen Aurora shook her head, and smiled a little knowing smile. "That wasn't *my* magic," she said. "I think it was something else."

"What?" asked the girls.

"The power of friendship," said Aurora. "It has a magic all of its own."

Aisha and Emily held hands. "We promise we'll *never* give up on Enchanted Valley," Emily said.

"Or on our friends," added Aisha.

"Yes, we never could have beaten Selena without Grubb and Spike!" said Spiritmane.

The gathered crowds burst out into wild cheering again. They showered Spike and Grubb with streamers, confetti and flower petals.

Grubb blushed. He went over to Queen Aurora.

"I'm sorry," he said. "I should never have helped Selena."

"That's OK," Queen Aurora said. "You're forgiven!"

"Am I?" Grubb said. "Wow. I mean …
thank you!"

Queen Aurora turned towards the
stadium. "Come along, everyone. Now we
have all the lockets back, the Enchanted
Valley Games can begin. It's time for the
opening ceremony!"

Chapter Eight
The Opening Ceremony Celebration

All the seats in the stadium were full.
From all across Enchanted Valley,
creatures had come to watch the fun.
Aisha and Emily sat in the front row, too
excited for words.

Queen Aurora's horn shimmered with

magic, and the sky turned a beautiful
dark blue.

Trumpets blew a fanfare. A single,
brilliant firework shot up and exploded
into a fountain of rainbow colours.
Suddenly, lights blazed all around the
stadium. The green turf in the middle had
been magically shaped into hills, valleys,
mountains and forests, complete with
rivers and lakes, and a very familiar-

looking model palace.

"It's a miniature Enchanted Valley!" Emily cried out.

Dancers came running in from all sides, representing every part of Enchanted Valley. The music changed to a happy jig, then to a swirling symphony, then to an exciting gallop. The girls watched goblins, dragons, mermaids, birds and – of course – unicorns, all putting on a spectacular

show. Spotlights shone on one part of the valley after another.

"They're showing us everything that makes the different places special!" Emily whispered to Aisha.

Ribbons and streamers danced in the air. Fireworks shimmered overhead. Then, after a final tremendous explosion of lights, silence fell.

Queen Aurora walked gracefully into the middle of the stadium. All the other unicorns came and stood with her in a circle.

The queen's horn began to glow. Multi-coloured lights went rippling up and down it. It grew brighter and brighter, lighting up the whole arena.

"I've never seen it shine so much," Aisha whispered.

Aurora leaned in close to the unicorn next to her and touched horns with them. The flaming glow passed from one horn to the other. That unicorn passed it to the next, and so it went on, from horn to horn all around the circle.

The last unicorn of all was a little foal.

She carried the fire up to a plinth, where a large crystal ball rested. She bowed her head and touched her horn to the ball.

The multi-coloured lights leapt into the crystal ball, which lit up and shone like a rainbow sun. The whole stadium was bathed in shimmering beauty. The sky changed back to daylight.

Spike whispered to the girls, "That's the Light of Friendship! It'll stay burning all through the Games. Everyone who sees it vill be reminded of what the Games are really about. Teamvork, confidence, sportsmanship and perseverance. And friendship, of course."

Quickhoof, Brightblaze, Fairtail and Spiritmane lined up in front of the plinth.

With one long blow on their golden whistles, the Games began!

Emily and Aisha lost count of all the events they saw. Every time one of their friends took part, they made sure to support them. Whether it was Fluffy the Cloud Puppy tumbling about with the other Cloud Puppies in a game of sky rugby, or their mermaid friend Pearl winning the upstream swimming race, or Hob the goblin trying his best in a floating chess match, they cheered and clapped.

When it was time for the hide and seek competition, both Spike and Grubb wanted to take part! All the hiders sprinted off to different corners of the

arena, while Queen Aurora closed her
eyes and counted.

Spike flew down and landed among the
goodies on the snack table. Aisha frowned
in confusion. "He's meant to be hiding,
not eating," she said.

But then, Spike rolled around in all the
flour and crumbs, and curled up next to
the bread rolls. With his light brown fur,
he looked just like another one!

"He's borrowed Grubb's trick!" laughed
Emily. "How clever."

Meanwhile, Grubb covered himself with
sand to hide in the long-jump pit.

"Ready or not, here I come!" Aurora
called.

Right away, she found a giggling little

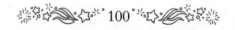

monkey beside her hoof. Then she spotted Hob, lying down beside the winners' podium. She  galloped happily around the stadium, finding more and more creatures.

Soon, only Spike and Grubb were left to find. The girls watched excitedly as Queen Aurora approached the snack table.

"Hmm," she said, bending over the cakes and pastries. "I wonder where they could be?"

Her long mane dangled over Spike.

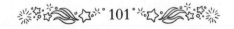

A moment later Spike burst into giggles and unrolled, sending flour everywhere. "It tickles!" he squeaked.

"Aha!" Queen Aurora said. "Found you!"

"That means Grubb is the winner," Aisha shouted. "Well done, Grubb!"

Grubb sat up in the sandpit. "What? I won? Really?"

"Congratulations!" Spike said. "Vot a brilliant hiding place, my friend. You deserved to vin!"

"But … aren't you sad that you lost?" Grubb asked nervously.

"Not at all!" beamed Spike. "I just love to play games with my friends."

Grubb grinned happily. "That's the

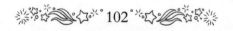

main thing, isn't it?"

Eventually, it was time for the
prizegiving. All the winners stood in line,
and Queen Aurora hung golden medals
around their necks, one by one. An
enormous cheer went up from the crowd.

Then the queen gave Grubb a special
laurel crown and named him Champion
of the Enchanted Valley Games!

"Sometimes the last ones to join the
team are
the ones
who make
the biggest
difference,"
she said with
a smile. "Now,

Aisha and Emily, would you please come up?"

The girls walked over to the winners' podium, a little confused. They hadn't played any of the games – why were they being called up?

Queen Aurora bent down and hung matching golden medals around their necks. "For saving Enchanted Valley," she explained, "and for never giving up!"

The whole stadium burst into applause. The girls looked out at their friends' grateful faces and smiled.

Emily and Aisha took their medals off, and they immediately shrank down into little golden charms. The girls added them to their keyrings along with the rest.

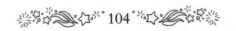

It was time to go home. The girls
hugged everybody goodbye.

"See you soon!" called Spike.

"Thanks again," added Grubb.

Aurora's horn glowed with a golden
light, and once again the multicoloured
sparkles rushed around them. Their feet
rose up off the ground …

… and came back down again on the

floor of the stationery cupboard, back at school.

They hurried back into their classroom. The clock on the wall was still at three. No time at all had passed while they'd been in Enchanted Valley. From outside came the bustling sounds of their classmates going home.

"Can we carry on looking for my unicorn pencil for a bit longer?" asked Emily. "I don't want to give up, after all."

"Definitely," Aisha said. "We should persevere!"

They began to search.

A moment later, Emily shouted for joy. "Aisha, look!"

On the classroom wall was a mural,

and parts of it were pink. Emily's unicorn pencil had fallen on to the floor and rolled up against one of the pink parts. Because the pencil was pink too, she hadn't seen it.

"It was camouflaged!" laughed Emily. "Just like Grubb."

"And Spike, all covered in flour," added Aisha.

Both girls smiled to think of their new friends, and all the fun they would have playing together.

They couldn't wait to go back to Enchanted Valley and see them again!

The End

Join Emily and Aisha
for more fun in …
**Sweetblossom
and the New Baby**
Read on for a sneak peek!

Aisha and Emily peeked out of the flap of their tent into the dark night. They wore the new onesies that they'd found laid out last night on their sleeping bags as a holiday surprise. Both onesies were covered in a unicorn print. Aisha's had a silver unicorn horn dangling from her hood. Emily's had a gold horn.

They'd arrived at Daffodil Dunes Campsite yesterday afternoon for a weekend away with Emily's parents. It was their first time camping and it had been such fun to sleep in a tiny tent all by themselves. They'd chattered long into the night over a midnight feast of chocolate chip cookies.

This morning's special treat was an exciting one. The four of them had agreed to wake up early to see the sun rise! Outside it was black right now, but they knew that soon the sun would peek over the horizon.

Read
Sweetblossom and the New Baby
**to find out what's in store
for Aisha and Emily!**

Also available

Book Nine:

Quickhoof and the Golden Cup

Book Ten:

Brightblaze Makes a Splash

Book Eleven:

Fairtail & the Perfect Puzzle

Book Twelve:

Spiritmane & the Hidden Magic

Unicorn Magic

Look out for the next book!

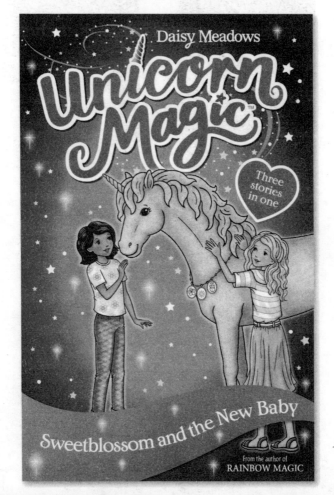

Daisy Meadows

Unicorn Magic™

Three stories in one

Sweetblossom and the New Baby

From the author of
RAINBOW MAGIC